Disney

Finding Tinker Bell

a Never Girls adventure

on the lost coast

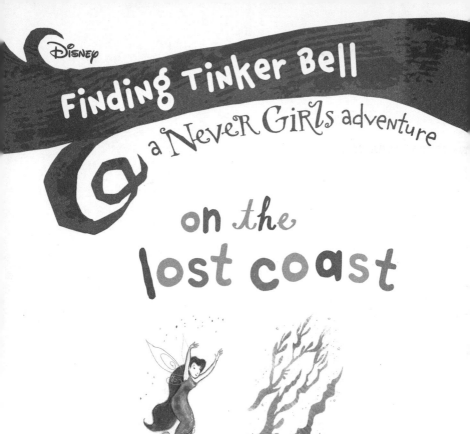

written by Kiki Thorpe

illustrated by Jana Christy

A STEPPING STONE BOOK™

RANDOM HOUSE 🏠 NEW YORK

For Lael —K.T.

Copyright © 2018 Disney Enterprises, Inc. All rights reserved. Published in the United States by Random House Children's Books, a division of Penguin Random House LLC, 1745 Broadway, New York, NY 10019, and in Canada by Penguin Random House Canada Limited, Toronto, in conjunction with Disney Enterprises, Inc. Random House and the colophon are registered trademarks and A Stepping Stone Book and the colophon are trademarks of Penguin Random House LLC.

Library of Congress Cataloging-in-Publication Data is available upon request.

ISBN 978-0-7364-3760-8 (trade) — ISBN 978-0-7364-9020-7 (lib. bdg.) — ISBN 978-0-7364-3761-5 (ebook)

rhcbooks.com

Printed in the United States of America

10 9 8 7 6 5 4 3 2 1

This book has been officially leveled by using the F&P Text Level Gradient™ Leveling System.

Never Land...
and Beyond

Far away from the world we know, on the distant Sea of Dreams, lies an island called Never Land. It is a place full of magic, where mermaids sing, fairies play, and children never grow up. Adventures happen every day, and anything is possible.

Though many children have heard of Never Land, only a special few ever find it. The secret, they know, lies not in a set of directions but deep within their hearts, for believing in magic can make extraordinary things happen. It can open doorways you never even knew were there.

One day, through an accident of magic, four special girls found a portal to Never Land right in their own backyard. The enchanted island became the girls' secret playground, one they visited every chance they got. With the fairies of Pixie Hollow as their friends and guides, they made many magical discoveries.

But Never Land isn't the only island on the Sea of Dreams. When a special friend goes missing, the girls set out across the sea to find her. Beyond the shores of Never Land, they encounter places far stranger than they ever could have imagined. . . .

This is their story.

Shadow Island

chapter 1

Kate McCrady took a deep breath and sighed. For what felt like the hundredth time that day, she climbed over a rotting log. She ducked under a giant fern. She tiptoed past a bunch of toadstools.

This is an adventure, Kate reminded herself. *Adventures are fun.*

Usually, Kate lived for adventures. She was lucky. At twelve, she'd had more of them than most people did in a lifetime.

That was because Kate and her friends had discovered a secret portal to Never Land. On that magical island, Kate had met dozens of fairies. She'd gone swimming in the Mermaid Lagoon. She'd flown through the sky, held up by nothing more than a bit of fairy dust and a breeze.

Now the girls' Never Land adventures had led them here, to the mysterious Shadow Island. They were looking for the fairy Tinker Bell, who had vanished a few days before. All clues suggested that Tink's disappearance had something to do with Shadow Island.

It should have been the greatest adventure yet. But at the moment, Kate was not having fun. Not even a little.

Kate was sweaty. She was tired. Worst

of all, she was bored. She was starting to have the sneaking suspicion that they were lost.

Kate shook her long red bangs out of her eyes. She wiped her damp brow with the back of her hand.

She called to the four fairies, who were leading the way. "Does anyone know where we're going?"

Four spots of light paused in the gloom.

"We're going to find Tink's boat," Fawn, the animal-talent fairy, replied. "I met an osprey who'd spotted it on the shore."

"But how do we *get* to the shore?" Kate asked.

The fairies looked at one another. "I'm following Iridessa," said the garden-talent fairy Rosetta.

"Well, *I'm* following Silvermist," Iridessa, the light-talent fairy, replied, pointing ahead.

"And I'm following Fawn," Silvermist, the water-talent fairy, said.

Fawn stared back at them in surprise. "I thought *you* were leading!"

"Ugh," Kate groaned. Her sneaking suspicion had turned into a certainty. "So we're totally lost."

Silvermist looked around. "I wouldn't say *totally*. . . ."

Kate frowned. "What *would* you say? Because *I'd* say we're going in circles in a dark forest on a strange, creepy island. And we have no idea where to find Tink or how to get home."

"When you put it that way, it does sound bad," Silvermist agreed.

"I need a break." As Kate sat down to rest on a tree stump, her friends Lainey Winters and Mia and Gabby Vasquez came straggling up. The girls looked as tired as Kate felt. Their shoulders sagged. Their feet scuffed the ground. Even Gabby's costume fairy wings looked droopy.

Lainey plopped down next to Kate. "I'm beat."

Mia and Gabby sat, too. The fairies flew down and landed on a tree stump.

Mia took off her shoes and rubbed her feet. "It feels like we've walked a hundred miles," she complained.

"Your feet wouldn't hurt if we were flying," Kate pointed out.

Mia sighed. "I know. But we need to save the fairy dust we have left. We don't know how long it will take to find Tink or get back to Never Land."

Kate knew Mia was right. When they'd left Pixie Hollow to search for Tinker Bell, they'd brought only a small amount of extra fairy dust. They hadn't known that they would end up so far away from Never Land.

Kate ran her fingers over the small bag in her pocket. Split between them, the fairy dust might only last a few days at most.

Without fairy dust, Kate and her friends couldn't fly. Without fairy dust, the fairies couldn't glow or do magic. They needed to find Tink soon.

"Gabby, do you still have that map?" Kate asked.

Gabby took the tiny scroll from her pocket and handed it to Kate. Gabby had found the map in Tinker Bell's workshop the day she'd gone missing. It was the first clue that Tink might be lost somewhere on Shadow Island.

Kate carefully unrolled the thin parchment and spread it across her knee.

The sketched ink drawing showed dense forest and a jagged coastline. But it was hard to tell where they were going when Kate couldn't even tell where they were.

Lainey leaned over her shoulder. She touched an area covered in cloud-like swirls. "What's that?"

Kate squinted at the tiny words written there. "'Lost Coast.' That's funny. I didn't notice that on the map before."

"What good is a magic map if it doesn't tell you where you are?" Rosetta grumbled.

Kate rolled up the map and started to hand it back to Gabby. Then she hesitated.

Gabby is only six. Can she be trusted to keep it safe? Kate wondered. "Maybe I should hold on to the map. For safekeeping," she suggested.

"*I'm* the one who found it," Gabby protested.

Kate opened her mouth to reply, then shrugged and handed the map back. It wasn't worth fighting over.

She stood and put her hands on her hips. She turned one way, then another. The forest looked the same in every direction.

"This way," Kate decided.

The fairies raised their eyebrows. "How do you know that's the right direction?" asked Iridessa.

"I don't," said Kate. "But we can't get more lost than we already are."

She set off. A moment later, she heard the flutter of fairy wings and the girls' footsteps behind her.

Gabby caught up with Kate. She had to double her pace to match Kate's stride. "I bet you guessed right, Kate," Gabby whispered.

Kate smiled down at her. She caught the smaller girl's hand and held it as they walked.

They hadn't gone far, when the air seemed to grow cooler. Silvermist's glow suddenly flared. "Do you smell that?" she asked.

They all sniffed the air. "I don't smell anything," Kate said.

"Me either," said Mia.

But Silvermist inhaled deeply. "It's salt water! I can smell the sea! Kate, you were right!"

She darted ahead. The girls scrambled

after her. Soon they could hear the *shush-shush* of rolling surf.

As they came through the trees, Kate stopped so suddenly that Lainey bumped into her. Together the girls and fairies stared in silence.

"Where are we?" Gabby asked.

chapter 2

They were on a beach. Fog lay thick over everything. Kate could hear waves rolling into shore, but she couldn't see them. The shapes of large rocks were the only things visible through the mist.

"Is this where we'll find the boat?" Gabby asked.

"It might be," Fawn said. "The osprey said he saw it on a beach."

"Let's look around," Kate said.

She took a step and immediately tripped on something. She bent to pick it up. "What the ...?"

It was a lunch box. Cartoon bears beamed at her from its side. They looked out of place in the gloom.

"What's a lunch box doing here?" Lainey asked.

"I don't know." Kate noticed other things scattered in the sand. A baseball cap. A ring of keys. A doll's arm. A pile of colorful socks stretched across the ground like a drift of seaweed.

Mia wrinkled her nose. "What is all this stuff?"

"It's probably just trash that washed ashore," Kate said. "Let's spread out. That way we'll cover more ground."

They fanned out along the beach. As Kate picked her way through the stuff, she noticed that it wasn't garbage of the usual sort. There were no fast-food cartons or plastic bags or busted car tires. Everything seemed like something someone would *want.* There were eyeglasses, combs, earrings, even a few wallets. But mostly Kate saw toys—teddy bears, toy soldiers, miniature cars, balls, and dolls of all shapes and sizes. The large shapes Kate had mistaken for rocks were actually piles of things. She felt as if she were walking through a yard sale—the strangest one ever.

Kate examined a kite with a long tail. It didn't have a single rip or tear. *Why would anyone throw this away?* she wondered.

As she set the kite down, Kate spotted a metal jack-in-the-box. Its once-colorful paint was chipped and faded.

"Hey! I had one like this when I was little." She grasped the tiny handle and gave it a turn.

With a musical tinkle, the lid popped open. A leering clown lunged out.

Kate jerked back, startled. Her foot landed on something that rolled, and she tumbled backward.

Kate got up, laughing. "Now I remember why I hated that toy." She looked around to see what she'd stepped on.

It was an old softball, scuffed and grass-stained. When she picked it up, it fit perfectly in her hand.

She turned it over, and her heart skipped a beat. There, in wobbly letters, was her own name. *Kate McCrady.*

It was her very first softball. She had written her name on it herself when she was five or six years old.

A memory suddenly came to Kate. She was standing in her backyard on a summer evening. The air smelled like mowed lawns and barbecues. "Hands up, Kate. Keep your eye on the ball," her father told her. She felt a satisfying *thunk* as the ball hit her mitt. It had been her first catch.

But she hadn't seen the ball in years. How had it ended up here?

A squeal came a few yards away.

"Gabby?" Still clutching her softball, Kate hurried toward the sound of the cry.

She found Gabby kneeling. The little girl's arms were squeezed tight against her chest. "What's wrong? Are you hurt?" Kate exclaimed.

"What happened?" Mia came running, with Lainey right behind her. She knelt down next to her sister. "Gabby, what is it?" she asked.

"I found my doggy," Gabby whispered.

Kate saw then that she wasn't doubled over in pain. She was cuddling something.

Mia's eyes opened wide. "Is that what I think it is?"

Gabby held up a bedraggled plush dog. Its matted fur had once been white but was now a dingy gray. It was missing one ear and its tail hung by a thread.

Mia looked as if she'd seen a ghost. "*BowBow?* I never thought we'd see him again."

"You lost him?" Kate asked.

"A long time ago," Mia said. "He was Gabby's favorite toy. She used to tie a string around his neck and drag him down the sidewalk like he was a real dog. One day, Mami put Gabby in the stroller. We didn't realize the string had come untied until we got home. We looked everywhere, but we never found him. Mami felt terrible about it."

"BowBow, I missed you." Gabby nuzzled the toy's grubby fur.

"I found my first softball," Kate told her friends. She held it out to show them her name.

The other girls stared. "What *is* this place?" Lainey asked.

"What's going on? Did you find the boat?" Iridessa darted over to them. Her glow was bright with excitement.

But when Kate and Gabby showed her their toys, the fairy's face fell. "I thought you'd found something *important.*"

"You don't understand," Kate said.

"These are important. They're *our* things. Things we lost."

Iridessa looked at her blankly. She *didn't* understand, but it wasn't her fault. The fairies of Never Land are born full-grown and stay that way their whole lives. They never outgrow their clothes or toys—or, for that matter, their wishes and dreams and silly ideas.

Simply put, fairies are who they have always been. And if they lose a beloved object, it's just gone—it doesn't take part of them with it.

So Iridessa had no way of seeing that when the girls found their lost toys, they were also finding pieces of their old selves.

"That's all fine," the light-talent fairy

said, "but we need to be looking for clues about Tink. We should have a system. Kate, you take the waterline. Mia, you search mid-beach. Lainey and Gabby, look at the high-tide mark. . . . "

But the girls weren't listening. They were scanning the beach with new interest. "The Lost Coast," Mia murmured.

"What's that?" Iridessa looked annoyed at being interrupted.

"The Lost Coast," Mia repeated. "This must be where lost things go."

"In that case," Iridessa said, "we should find Tink in no time." She buzzed off, her wings whirring like a hummingbird's.

The girls spread out again. This time Kate went slowly. She examined everything—thermos bottles, plastic dinosaurs, wooden buttons, glass marbles.

In a tangle of socks, Kate spotted a pattern that sent a jolt right through her.

"Ellie?"

She fished a little calico elephant out of the pile. It had black button eyes and an embroidered smile. The fabric of its trunk was shiny from where it had been rubbed a thousand times.

The toy looked older than Kate remembered, but it was still the elephant she had once loved. Her first best friend. Memories flickered through Kate's mind. Sleeping with Ellie. Reading to Ellie. Tricycle rides with Ellie in her basket. Holding Ellie up to look out the open car window—and the awful moment Ellie had fallen from her hand.

Kate lifted the toy to her nose and breathed in. Ellie smelled as she always had—like sleep and dust and sunshine. For a moment Kate felt as if she were three years old again, snug under the covers with Ellie by her side.

Kate tucked the elephant into the crook of her arm next to the softball. Not far away, Mia gasped as she pulled something from a pile. Kate wondered what she'd found. Knowing Mia, it was something pretty—an old doll or a bracelet.

A dull gleam in the sand caught Kate's eye. She sifted out a handful of coins and pocketed them. Maybe they were hers. Maybe they weren't. But she was always losing her lunch money at school.

Kate hurried hopefully to the next

pile. The more she found, the more she wanted to find. It was like being on an endless Easter egg hunt. There were so many treasures to find—she just had to keep looking.

chapter 3

Silvermist shivered in the fog. She had been searching for some time, but she hadn't seen any sign of Tinker Bell or the missing boat.

Even if the boat is here, I doubt we'll find it in this mess, she thought.

Silvermist darted down to another pile of junk. She flew past a toy car, a single glove, a polka-dot umbrella, a tennis racket, a whole baby carriage. . . .

Silvermist paused, then peeped inside. The carriage was empty.

Phew! She sighed in relief.

Why did Clumsies need so much stuff? Silvermist didn't understand it. In Pixie Hollow there was just the right amount of everything—no more, no less. Was having too many things what made people so careless with them?

Silvermist sighed and moved on. Normally, she loved being near the ocean. But this beach had such a sad, lonely feeling. She hoped they'd find Tinker Bell soon. She didn't want to spend any more time in this strange place.

"Nothing over here," she called to her friends. "Let's try a little farther down the beach."

There was no answer. Suddenly, Silvermist realized she couldn't see any of the other fairies' glows.

"Fawn?" she called. "Rosetta? Dessa?"

She strained her ears. The only sound was the *hush-hush* of waves.

Which way had they gone? Right or left? Silvermist flitted back and forth, trying to make up her mind. She was afraid to go too far in any direction in case it was the wrong way. She might never find her way back in the thick fog.

Just then, she spotted a small figure coming through the mist.

"Gabby! Thank goodness!" Silvermist darted toward her.

She was a foot or two away when she realized the

thing coming toward her wasn't Gabby. She wasn't even sure it was human.

Silvermist froze. She looked around for a place to hide, but it was too late. Whatever it was had surely seen her glow. Silvermist braced herself as the creature emerged from the mist.

He was the size of a small child, but stouter. From his extra-long, knobby nose, Silvermist guessed he was some kind of troll. He was dressed in an assortment of odd items—a tinsel garland, mismatched rain boots, an embroidered tea cozy on his head. He moved slowly, humming to himself. He didn't see Silvermist until he almost bumped into her.

"Eeep!" the troll screamed, jumping a foot in the air.

He glared at Silvermist from beneath the tea cozy.

"What's the meaning of this, sneaking up on me like that?" he huffed.

"I didn't mean to scare you," Silvermist said. "I thought you were someone else."

The troll harrumphed and straightened his tinsel. "Where did you come from?"

"I'm not sure. I think I'm lost," Silvermist told him.

"Of course you're lost!" the troll said with a snort. "Why else would you be here?"

"I don't understand," said Silvermist.

"This is the Lost Coast, home to the mislaid and the cast away. If it can't be found, you'll find it here. And if it's here, it's surely lost." The troll narrowed his eyes at her. "First-time visitor?"

Silvermist nodded.

"You'll soon get used to it. I myself have been lost for . . ." He scratched his head. "Well, I've lost count of the days. But it's been quite a while!"

"Maybe you can help me?" Silvermist asked. "I can't seem to find my way in all this fog—"

The troll shook his head. "I wouldn't bother trying to find *that.*"

"Trying to find what?" asked Silvermist.

"Your way," said the troll. "Slippery things, ways. Always turning hither and thither. This-a-way, that-a-way. It's no wonder so many folks get lost following them. I lost my way years ago, and quite frankly, I'm better off without it."

"Oh dear." Silvermist rubbed her

forehead. The troll seemed to be talking in riddles. "I'm just looking for my friends. They're around here somewhere. Could you help me find them?"

"That depends," said the troll. "Are they lost, too?"

"I don't think so," Silvermist said. "We got separated is all."

"Then I'm afraid I can't help," said the troll. "If they're not lost, then we certainly won't find them."

Silvermist sighed. Everything the troll said only confused her more. "Thank you anyway."

"Anytime," the troll said pleasantly. He seemed to have forgotten he was annoyed. "It's been ever so nice chatting. But I have things to do and places to be."

He tipped his tea cozy at Silvermist and shuffled off into the fog.

"What an odd fellow," Silvermist said to herself. "But what am I going to do now?"

She decided she had better retrace her steps. She began to fly slowly back over the pile—past the empty baby carriage,

around the tennis racket, over the umbrella, the glove. . . .

A creeping feeling made her pause. She glanced behind her.

At first she couldn't see anything wrong. Then she realized—

The umbrella was gone!

She flew back to the spot. There had been an umbrella, hadn't there? She saw it clearly in her mind's eye—a green umbrella with bright pink dots. But it wasn't there now.

No one had come. No wind had stirred. The umbrella had simply vanished.

Silvermist shivered. She felt a chill that had nothing to do with the fog. She didn't think she could stand to be alone a moment longer.

"Wait!" she called to the troll, flying in the direction he had gone. "Oh, wait for me, please!"

chapter 4

"Mr. Troll?" Silvermist flew through the swirling fog. "Hello?"

Just when she thought she'd lost him for good, she spotted him scuffling along. Silvermist darted up to him. "There you are!"

"Eeep!" the troll screamed, and flailed his arms.

"Oh dear." Silvermist sighed. "Don't you remember me? We just met."

"Did we?" The troll squinted at her.

"So we did! Forgive me, I was lost in my thoughts."

Silvermist smiled. "I get lost in my thoughts sometimes, too. Do you mind if I fly with you?"

"Be my guest," said the troll. He began to walk again, resuming his humming. He kept losing the melody. He always reached the same point, then started over.

"By the way, I forgot to ask your name," Silvermist said.

The troll's mouth turned down. "There's no need to be rude."

"Goodness. I didn't mean to offend you!" Silvermist said, startled.

"I don't ask *you* snooty questions," the troll said. "'Who are you?' and 'Where do you come from?' and so on."

"I wouldn't mind if you did," the fairy

replied. "I'm Silvermist. I come from Pixie Hollow on the island of Never Land."

"You needn't rub it in," the troll sniffed.

"Haven't you got a home?" Silvermist asked.

"Did once," the troll said gruffly. "Haven't been able to locate it recently."

"And your name?" Silvermist asked.

"Also misplaced," the troll mumbled.

Silvermist's heart went out to the poor creature. "And is that how you ended up here? You got lost?"

"Oh no," said the troll. "You've got it backward. I'm not lost. I always know where I am. It's everything else that's gone astray."

"I see," said Silvermist, though she didn't really.

"I'm always losing things," the troll

went on. "I've lost hours of time. Lost my nerve. Once I lost my voice for a whole week. I don't know where it went, but it was never the same after I found it again. That's why I stay here. If I wander around long enough, I'm bound to bump into something I'm looking for. But what about you?" the troll asked. "How did you come to be on the Lost Coast?"

"I'm looking for a boat," said Silvermist.

"Plenty of those turn up here," the troll said. "What sort of boat is it? Schooner? Catamaran? Submarine?"

"It's a little boat, actually," Silvermist said. "A small green boat no bigger than your arm. Just the size for a fairy."

The troll brightened. "I've seen a boat like that!"

"You have?" Silvermist exclaimed. "Can

you show me where you saw it?"

"Certainly," said the troll. "Follow me!"

He veered to the left, moving quickly in his mismatched boots. Silvermist had to flap her wings double-time to keep up with him. Her heart raced. Could Tink be somewhere just ahead?

"It's not only the boat I'm looking for," Silvermist explained. "My friend Tinker Bell was sailing it. She left Pixie Hollow a few days ago, and no one has seen her since. My friends and I have come to rescue her."

"Ah, she's the helpless sort," the troll said.

"Tink? Helpless?" Silvermist laughed. "Far from it! She's one of the cleverest fairies I know. She's stubborn, too. She never gives up."

"Then why are you worried about her?"

the troll asked. "She sounds like she'll do fine on her own."

"Because she's missing," said Silvermist. "And she's my friend."

The troll nodded. "A friend is the worst thing to lose. Well, here we are."

"Here?" Silvermist looked around. They'd come to a sand spit that reached like an arm into the ocean. Unlike the rest of the beach, it was clean and uncluttered.

Silvermist scanned the smooth stretch of sand. "There's nothing here. Are you sure this is the right place?"

The troll looked around. "It *was* here."

"Where could it have gone?" Silvermist thought of the vanished umbrella, and her stomach dipped.

"It hasn't *gone* anywhere," the troll said. "I'd guess it's been found."

"Found? By whom?" Silvermist asked.

"Who knows? All I can tell you is that if it's been found, it's lost to us."

"Oh, never mind." Silvermist didn't want any more of the troll's riddles. The bubble of hope inside her burst. A tear slid down her cheek.

"There, there," the troll said. He pulled a woolen sock from his pocket and held it out like a handkerchief.

Silvermist dried her eyes on the toe. "I don't know what to do. I can't find my friends. I don't know which way to go."

"Try following your nose. That's how I get about." The troll crossed his eyes and looked at the tip of his nose.

"But how do you see where you're going?" Silvermist asked.

"I don't," the troll said. "But this way I always know where I am."

The troll said good-bye. Then he set off into the mist. "Just remember," he called back to Silvermist. "If it's lost, you'll surely find it here..." His voice faded away before she could hear the rest.

Silvermist rubbed her arms. It was awful to be alone in this place.

Except...

All of a sudden, Silvermist knew she was not alone. Someone was following her.

She spun around. No one was there.

But wait...a dark blur in the mist sharpened into a familiar silhouette. It had a high bun, wings, and a short leaf-dress.

Silvermist gasped. "Tinker Bell?"

The figure in the mist gave a start, as if it had been caught. Then it turned and fled.

"Tink!" Silvermist cried, chasing after her. "Wait! Come back!"

chapter 5

"Kate? What are you doing?"

The question seemed to come to Kate from miles away. Slowly, as if waking from a dream, Kate dragged her gaze away from her lap. The fairy Rosetta hovered before her, frowning.

Kate glanced back down at the stack of comic books in her lap. "I'm looking for Wonder Woman. I had this great Wonder

Woman comic book, only I can't find it."

Rosetta's frown deepened. "Are you feeling all right?"

Come to think of it, Kate did feel sort of strange. Like she'd been asleep. "How long have I been sitting here?" she asked.

"A long time," Rosetta said. "Hours, maybe. We've searched this whole place, but there's no sign of Tink or the boat. We need to move on."

Kate rose, noticing that her legs felt stiff. "Hold on. Let me get my things," she said.

Still clutching the comic books, Kate stood and picked up Ellie. She tucked the elephant back into the crook of her arm, along with her softball and a few books she'd checked out of the school library six months before. But it was too much to hold. The softball slipped from her arm. When she tried to pick it up, she dropped Ellie.

Rosetta's foot tapped the air impatiently. "Leave those things."

"No," said Kate. "Just give me a minute." She stooped to pick up Ellie and dropped a book. Kate looked around. A blue backpack lay on the sand nearby. She picked it up and brushed it off. It didn't belong to her. But it was already lost. Whoever it belonged to wouldn't miss it more if she took it.

Finders keepers, Kate told herself.

She loaded the backpack, stuffing it with her toys, books, and other things she'd found on the Lost Coast. By the time she was through, she could barely close the zipper.

She swung the backpack heavily onto her back and followed Rosetta to where the other girls and fairies were. Even before they reached them, Kate could hear raised voices.

"We can't bring all that!" Iridessa was saying.

"Why not? *We're* the ones carrying it," came Mia's reply.

As Kate emerged from the fog, she saw what they were talking about. Mia, Lainey, and Gabby were surrounded by piles of things. Dolls, games, and clothes, which looked much too small, sat in a basket at Mia's feet. Lainey held a pillowcase full of stuffed animals. Gabby's arms were also full of toys, including BowBow. A baby blanket was tied around her neck like a cape.

"I can't leave *her* behind." Mia thrust out a giant plastic doll with tangled hair. "She was my favorite doll in first grade. And I found my journal from second grade. And my rainbow hat—"

"I *need* BowBow," Gabby added. "And my blankie and my squeaky giraffe and this rubber ducky . . ."

"What about you? Those can't *all* be yours." Iridessa eyed the stuffed animals in Lainey's pillowcase.

"Not all of them," Lainey admitted. "But they looked so lonely. I just couldn't leave them behind."

"It's our stuff," Kate spoke up. "We can take it if we want to."

"But we're not here to find *things*," Iridessa protested. "We need to stay focused on finding Tinker Bell—"

"And the boat," Gabby reminded her. "I'm not leaving without our great-grandpa's boat."

"And the boat." Iridessa nodded. "But bringing all that other stuff will only slow us down."

"Could you leave *some* of it behind?" Rosetta asked the girls.

"No!" they chorused.

The girls glared at the fairies. The fairies glared back.

Kate couldn't say exactly what came over her at that moment. But with a quick motion, she undid the pouch on her belt. She snatched up a handful of fairy dust and tossed it over the piles of things.

"There!" she snapped. "*Now* they won't slow us down."

The fairies gasped. The other girls looked shocked. Kate felt a little shocked herself.

"The fairy dust!" Rosetta exclaimed.

"I can't believe you did that," Iridessa said.

Kate squared her jaw. "Well, it's done." She hoisted the full backpack onto her shoulder again. The fairy dust made it feel as light as a feather.

But before they could go anywhere,

Fawn dashed up. She looked worried. "We have another problem. I can't find Silvermist."

On another part of the beach, Silvermist raced after Tinker Bell. Or what she thought was Tink, anyway. The shape in the mist looked just like her friend. But why was Tink running away?

"Tink, stop! Why won't you talk to me?" Silvermist called.

The shape zigzagged like a fish trying to shake free from a hook. Silvermist's wings were starting to get tired. She struggled to keep up.

There was something odd about the way Tink looked. She had no glow!

The thought drew Silvermist up short, and just in time. For a wall of rock loomed out of the fog. If she hadn't stopped right then, Silvermist would have slammed into it.

The sheer wall rose so high she couldn't see the top. The only opening was a single hairline crack too small for a fairy to fit

through. Silvermist searched for a way around it. She found none.

The Tink-like shape was gone. It had vanished like a wisp of smoke.

What was I following? Silvermist wondered. Was it a spirit pretending to look like her friend? Or was her own mind playing tricks on her?

Back in Pixie Hollow, Silvermist had heard tales about Shadow Island. It was said to be a cursed place where nothing was as it seemed. But they were only stories, meant to give fairies the shivers. Silvermist hadn't imagined they might be true.

Then again, she hadn't imagined Shadow Island was real, either.

Voices floated toward her. She heard the

silvery tones of a fairy speaking, followed by the rise and fall of a girl's voice.

"I can't believe you did that."

"Well, it's done."

Silvermist hesitated, afraid to trust her ears. But the voices sounded real, so she followed them.

"Oh thank goodness—" Silvermist broke off when she saw her friends. From the looks on their faces, she could tell something bad had happened.

"Here's Silvermist!" Kate said tensely. "See, there's nothing to worry about."

"Where were you?" Fawn asked, fluttering over to her.

"I—" Silvermist shook her head. She didn't know where to begin. "What's going on here?"

"Nothing," Kate said firmly. "We were just saying it's time to get off this beach. Everybody ready?"

Without waiting for an answer, Kate charged off. The other girls exchanged glances. Then they picked up their things and started after her.

"What happened? Why is everyone upset?" Silvermist whispered to Fawn.

Fawn told Silvermist about the fairy dust. "It was like Kate lost her mind for a moment. I've never seen her act like that."

It's this place, Silvermist thought. *It makes everything strange.* She was glad they would soon be leaving the Lost Coast.

chapter 6

For a while, they trudged in silence. Though their loads were light, the air between them felt heavy. Kate couldn't help but notice the sour mood.

Why had she grabbed the fairy dust like that? Kate didn't know. Something had just come over her. She hadn't stopped to think about it until it was done.

There's no use crying over spilled fairy dust, Kate told herself. *Someone had to take charge. We weren't getting anywhere by just talking.*

Still, their search wasn't fun with everyone moping. She wished she could do something to lighten the mood.

Kate stopped and turned to the group. "Hey, why don't we take a break and have something to eat?"

"Great idea, Kate," Mia said. "But you're forgetting one thing—we don't have any *food*."

"Oh no?" Kate reached inside her backpack. She pulled out a banana.

Seven mouths fell open in surprise. "Where did you get that?" Lainey asked.

"The lunch boxes!" Kate said with a grin.

"You got that out of somebody's old lunch box? Ew!" Mia wrinkled her nose.

"Not old," Kate said. "Some of them

must have been lost pretty recently. The food was still fresh."

Gabby spread her baby blanket on the ground, and the group happily sat down for a picnic.

Mia and Lainey split a peanut butter sandwich, while the fairies helped themselves to a small box of raisins. Gabby shared bites of her banana with BowBow the stuffed dog.

"Couldn't you find any cookies, Kate?" Gabby asked through a mouthful. "Or a chocolate bar?"

Kate shook her head. "Not a single one."

"No dessert? That's weird," said Lainey.

"No, it isn't," Mia said. "Think about it. What's the first thing *you* eat from your lunch box?"

"Dessert!" the other girls chorused.

Listening to their laughter, Kate smiled. How smart she'd been to look in the lunch boxes! No one else had thought of that.

As they ate, Silvermist told them about her encounter with the troll. "He was a funny fellow. He couldn't even tell me his name. He said he'd lost it."

"Sounds to me like he lost his *marbles*," said Kate.

"He swore he'd seen Tink's boat," Silvermist went on. "He took me to the exact spot, but it wasn't there. When I asked where it could have gone, he said, 'It hasn't gone anywhere. It's been *found*.'"

"What does that mean?" Rosetta asked.

"I'm not sure," Silvermist admitted.

"Maybe Tink landed there, then decided she didn't want to stay and sailed on," Lainey said.

Mia narrowed her eyes. "Or maybe *we* were the ones who found it."

Everyone looked at her. "What are you talking about?" asked Kate.

Mia gestured to their toys. "Everything in this place is something that's been lost and forgotten about. The boat Tink was sailing was forgotten, too—but only until *we* found it."

"We found it in our *basement*," Gabby reminded her.

"Exactly," said Mia. "Once we found it, it wasn't lost anymore. And once it wasn't lost, it wasn't here."

"Mia, nothing you say makes sense," Kate told her. "How could the boat have been here if it was in your basement the whole time?"

"Do we know it was always there?" Mia asked. "How do you know something is there if you can't see it? Maybe the boat was *here* until we were ready to find it."

Lainey rubbed her temples. "Just thinking about that makes my brain hurt."

"Whether or not Tink was ever on the beach, what we know for sure is that she's not here now," Iridessa said. "We've searched this whole beach, and there's no sign of her."

"Except one." Silvermist hesitated, as if she wasn't sure she should tell them. "I thought I saw Tink. But she ran away from me." She lowered her voice to a whisper. "And the strangest thing was, she didn't have a *glow*."

The group fell silent. What could it mean?

As they'd been talking, the fog had turned from white to gray. The daylight was fading. Iridessa fluttered up from the blanket, brightening her glow. "We need to get off this beach. It's going to be dark soon. We can spend the night in the forest. The trees will shelter us."

They quickly collected their things. The fairies led the way. The fog had grown even thicker, but the fairies' light made them easy to follow.

They hadn't been walking for long when Kate realized that Gabby was no longer beside her.

"Gabby?" Kate stopped and turned. She went back a few paces and found Gabby. She was searching for something on the ground.

"I dropped BowBow!" Gabby cried.

"Don't worry. I'll help you find him." Kate cast an anxious glance toward the bobbing lights. She didn't want to fall too far behind. "Wait for us!" she called.

Kate kicked her feet through the

sand. The fog made it difficult to see the ground, but she finally glimpsed a bit of dingy fur. "There he is!" Kate plucked BowBow out of the sand and handed him to Gabby.

Gabby hugged the dog tightly.

"Come on," Kate said. "Let's hurry and catch up."

But when she looked back the way she'd come, she could no longer see the fairies' glow.

Kate spun around. In the opposite direction, she spied a glimmer in the growing darkness.

"I must have gotten mixed up. This way!" she told Gabby.

The two girls hurried toward the spots of light. *There's something odd about the way they're moving,* Kate thought. They looked as if they were dancing. Why would the fairies be dancing?

The sand grew wet beneath their feet. The sound of the surf was louder. Kate could tell they were close to the water's edge. But still the lights danced on.

"Silvermist?" Kate called. "Iridessa? Wait for us!"

She heard murmuring. The words were unclear, but they had the silvery tones of fairy voices.

"Why aren't they stopping?" Gabby asked.

"They must not hear us," Kate said. "Come on."

They had come to a pile of boulders that formed a natural jetty. The lights hovered just beyond it.

"Rosetta?" Kate called. "Fawn? Mia?

Where are you going? Can you hear me?"

In reply, she heard more fairy jingles. What were they saying? Why didn't the fairies come back for them?

Kate and Gabby began to climb toward the lights. The rocks were wet and slimy with seaweed. Twice Kate's foot slid.

"Take my hand," she told Gabby.

Together they inched across the slippery rocks. A wave crashed against the boulders, soaking their sneakers. Another drenched their legs in spray.

Then Kate heard a voice as clear as a bell. "Kate! Gabby! *Stop!*"

The girls froze. A second later, a wave crashed across the rock in front of them. If they'd been there, the water would have swept them away.

They heard the beat of tiny wings, and

a fairy appeared. In the mist, her glow looked like a halo.

"Silvermist!" cried Kate. "But I thought . . ." She looked back at the wavering lights and felt a shiver of fear.

"They're sea wraiths," Silvermist said. "Nothing good comes of following them."

"But they sound exactly like fairies!" Gabby said.

"They can mimic sound," Silvermist replied. "They probably heard us on the beach. They imitated our voices."

"Will they hurt us?" Kate was suddenly aware of how far they were from shore.

"Not now," Silvermist said. "But many people have gotten lost at sea chasing after them. It's a good thing we came looking for you when we did."

With Silvermist guiding them, Kate and Gabby slowly made their way back over the rocks. They found Mia and Lainey plus the other fairies waiting on the beach. They all looked worried.

"We'd better stop for the night," Iridessa said. "It's too risky to keep going in the dark. We'll try again in the morning."

Kate didn't like the idea of sleeping there, with the sea wraiths so near. But she was too tired to argue.

The girls bedded down, using stuffed animals as pillows. The fairies dug little holes in the sand. They folded their wings over themselves like blankets.

Kate's body felt exhausted. But even cuddling Ellie didn't help her fall asleep. Something was bothering her.

"Mia?" she whispered.

"Mmm?" came her friend's sleepy voice.

"That thing you were saying before, about Tink's boat. You said only lost things end up on the Lost Coast, right?"

"That's right," Mia said.

"I just realized something," Kate said. "Tinker Bell isn't here. But *we* are."

chapter 7

That night, Kate tossed and turned in her sleep, dreaming of dancing lights. In the morning, she awoke to a new world. She sat up with a gasp, blinking.

The fog had finally lifted. Sand stretched far in either direction, ending at tall cliffs. Sunlight sparkled on the waves of the greenish sea.

As the sun warmed her skin, the day before seemed like a bad dream. *Today will be better,* Kate told herself. Today they would discover something new. Maybe they would find Tink and return to Never Land. Their journey would become the adventure it was supposed to be.

"Oh geez," said Mia.

Kate glanced over. Mia was awake, but she wasn't taking in the view. She was watching Gabby.

The little girl lay asleep on her blanket. One arm was wrapped around BowBow. The thumb of the other hand was in her mouth.

"She looks sweet," said Kate.

"It's not that," said Mia. "She's sucking her thumb. She hasn't done that since she was four."

"She's probably just tired," Kate said.

"I guess." Mia frowned. "It's just that she worked so hard to stop." As if she couldn't

stand to watch any longer, she gave Gabby a little shake. "Gabby, time to wake up."

"Mami? Oh." Gabby sat up, blinking as she remembered where she was. "Did we find Tink?"

Kate laughed. "Not yet, Gabby. But today may be our lucky day!"

They woke up Lainey and the fairies,

who took in their surroundings one by one.

"That's strange," Fawn said, gazing at the tall cliffs. "Where's the forest?"

"What do you mean?" Mia asked.

"We came here through a forest," Fawn said. "But there's no forest now. The only way out of here is over those cliffs."

Kate saw what she meant. The cliffs hemmed them in like the walls of a fortress. Kate had the strange impression they'd sprung up overnight.

But of course, that wasn't possible. "We must have come around a point or something," Kate said. "Maybe we passed them in the fog without realizing it. The question is, where to next?"

"I think we should retrace our path,"

Rosetta said. "We can talk to the sprites who live in the forest again. They know the island better than we do. Maybe they'll have another idea where to look for Tink."

Bor-ing! Kate thought. She didn't want another day of plodding through the forest. "Any other ideas?"

Gabby had moved to the edge of the water. She pointed toward the horizon. "What's that?"

In the distance, towers and spires rose above the water.

Mia gasped. "A castle!"

"A *huge* castle," added Lainey.

"A *magic* castle," whispered Gabby.

They all gazed at the strange building. It seemed to shimmer in the morning light.

"Who lives there?" Gabby wondered.

"There's only one way to find out!" Kate said.

Iridessa looked surprised. "You don't think we should go there?"

"I do!" said Kate. "Maybe whoever lives there can help us." *It's a magic castle!* she added to herself. *How could they not go?*

"What if they aren't friendly?" Rosetta asked.

"We'll fly in from above," Kate said. "If it looks dangerous, we'll retreat." This adventure was looking better by the minute.

"But what about the sea wraiths?" asked Fawn.

"We know to watch out for them now," Kate said.

"It looks far," Iridessa argued. "It would take a lot of fairy dust to fly there."

"I agree with Iridessa," said Fawn. "We'd be better off sticking to the shore."

Kate gritted her teeth in frustration. Why were the fairies being so difficult? She could feel her chance at adventure slipping away. One look at the other girls told her they felt the same.

"Let's vote on it," Kate said. "Who thinks we should go to the castle? Raise your hand."

The four girls' hands shot up.

"And who thinks we *shouldn't* go?" Kate asked.

Iridessa, Rosetta, and Fawn raised their hands. Silvermist raised her hand. Then she lowered it. Then she raised it halfway.

Iridessa rolled her eyes. "Silvermist, make up your mind."

"Okay." Silvermist raised her hand.

"It's a tie." Mia sighed. "So now what do we do?"

"I know how to settle this." Kate dug a coin from her pocket. "Heads, we go to the castle. Tails, we stay on the shore. Fair enough?"

The girls and fairies glanced at each other. One by one they nodded.

Kate flipped the coin. They watched it rise in the air, spinning end over end.

When the coin fell, Kate caught it.

Everyone leaned in. Slowly, Kate opened her hand.

"Heads!" she declared. "We go to the castle."

"I still think we'd be better off in the forest," Rosetta grumbled.

"Time for fairy dust!" Cheerfully, Kate pulled the bag from her pocket.

She paused before opening it. There was much less dust than she'd thought. Kate remembered that was her fault.

"Is everything okay?" Mia asked.

"Oh. Sure," Kate said. She took a tiny pinch between her fingers, letting extra grains of dust fall back into the bag. "Here, Mia. You're first." She sprinkled the bit of dust over Mia's head and shoulders, then doled out equally small pinches to the rest of the group.

"Save some for the trip back," Iridessa warned.

"Mm-hmm." Kate cinched the bag closed and returned it to her pocket. There wasn't much fairy dust left. But surely they could make it last.

Kate put the problem out of her mind and focused on the trip ahead. The fairy-dust magic was already working. Her feet started to rise off the ground.

She picked up her backpack. It was heavier than the day before.

The fairy dust must have worn off, she thought. *Oh well. It's nothing I can't handle.*

As Kate swung the backpack onto her shoulder, she realized she was still holding the coin. It was an old tarnished piece of silver. The features of the face on the engraved head were worn away.

Kate turned it over. The profile of a woman decorated the other side.

The coin had two heads! It hadn't been a fair coin toss after all.

"Hey, guys . . . ?" Kate began. But the fairies had already lifted off. They were too far away to hear her.

Oh well, Kate thought. *We made a decision. That was the point, wasn't it?*

Pocketing the coin, she rose into the air and flew after them.

chapter 8

High over the water, Kate took a deep breath of salty sea air. This was where she was happiest, up soaring on the wind. Not plodding along the ground like some old donkey.

The sun beat down on her head. But the breeze off the water was cool. For a while, Kate led the way. A tailwind helped her along. *At this rate, we'll be there in no time,* she thought.

An ache started between Kate's shoulder blades. At first it was just an annoying pinch. But as the heavy backpack dragged on her, the pinch soon turned into a cramp. Then the cramp turned into a burn.

How much farther? Kate scanned the horizon. Far off, the castle wavered in the air. It didn't look any closer than when they'd started.

Kate was sweating now. The sun glared in her eyes. She began to fly slower. If they didn't find a place to rest soon, she was going to be in trouble.

Just then, she spotted a small island below in the water. Kate beelined toward it. The other girls landed, too, tossing down their things with groans of relief. The fairies fluttered down to join them.

"Flying seems harder than usual today," Lainey remarked.

"I feel extra heavy," Mia agreed.

Kate said nothing, and instead looked around the small island. It wasn't much more than a large, dome-shaped rock. Wind and sea had carved an odd hexagonal pattern into its surface. Other than that, there was nothing to be seen. Not a house or a tree, not even a bush.

"How much farther?" Gabby asked. "I don't think I can fly much more."

Mia squinted at the faraway castle. "It doesn't look any closer than when we started. If I didn't know better, I'd swear it was moving away from us."

Iridessa jumped up as if she'd been stung. "Wait—what did you say?"

"I said it seems as if it's moving away

from us," Mia repeated, confused.

Iridessa clasped her tiny hands to her cheeks. "Oh no! Why didn't I think of it before?"

"Think of what?" asked Lainey.

The light-talent fairy didn't reply. She zipped high into the air over their heads and hovered there. Then she swooped down toward the sea. She flew a slow circle, skimming the surface of the water.

"Is she okay?" Gabby asked. The other fairies shrugged.

Iridessa flew back to them. Her face looked grim.

"There is no castle," she told them. "It's a mirage."

"How do you know?" Lainey asked.

"The air by the water is cool," Iridessa explained. "The air above is warmer. When that happens, light bends in a funny way. What we thought was a castle was probably more cliffs. A trick of light made them seem bigger than they are."

"I can't believe it!" Kate said. The castle had looked so real!

Iridessa put her hands on her hips.

"Believe me. I'm a light fairy. I know these things."

"It's okay," Mia said. "We still have fairy dust left. We'll just fly back to shore and figure out where to go next."

"Er, right." Slowly, Kate took the bag of fairy dust from her pocket, praying there was enough left. But as she started to open it, the entire island gave a sudden shudder.

The bag fell from her hand. It rolled down the steep side of the rock and fell into the water.

"The fairy dust!" Mia cried.

All four fairies darted toward the bag. Before they could reach it, the water next to the island started to bubble and churn.

As they watched in horror, a huge leathery head emerged from the water. The creature opened its mouth . . . and swallowed the bag of fairy dust!

chapter 9

Silvermist and the other fairies watched the small bag disappear.

"Our fairy dust!" Iridessa dove foward as if she might still save the bag. But there was nothing she could do. The dust was gone.

Another tremor shook the ground beneath the girls' feet. "What's happening to the island?" Mia cried.

"Oh no!" Suddenly, Silvermist realized

why the rock looked so strange. "This is no island!"

The giant head swiveled around just as the girls realized they were standing on the back of a monstrous tortoise. They tried to rise into the air. But they couldn't. They'd used up their fairy dust.

Discomfort crossed the tortoise's wizened face. He opened his mouth and hiccupped. His shell jerked and trembled, rocking the girls.

"Hold on!" Silvermist called to them. "We'll help you!"

Even as the words left her mouth, she wondered what they could do. They were only tiny fairies. How could they save four girls who were ten times their size?

We might be small, but we still have magic,

Silvermist reminded herself. She turned to Fawn. "You speak Tortoise, don't you? Can you talk to him?"

"I'll try!" Fawn swooped closer to the tortoise's face. She was a speck next to his enormous head. Silvermist could see Fawn waving her arms, though she couldn't hear what she was saying.

The tortoise gazed at Fawn and slowly

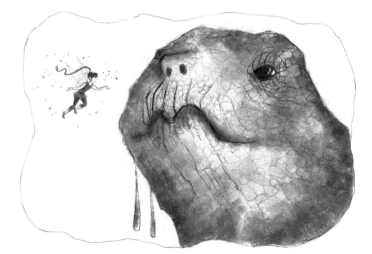

blinked. Then he opened his mouth and hiccupped.

Fawn flew back to the fairies. "It's not working," she said. "Tortoises don't hear well, and this one's deafer than most. From the look of him, he could be thousands of years old."

Another huge hiccup rocked the tortoise. It knocked the girls off their feet. They clung to the ridges on his shell to keep from sliding off his back.

"His hiccups are getting worse!" Rosetta said.

"It must be the fairy dust," said Fawn. "It's giving him indigestion."

"The girls aren't going to be able to hold on much longer," said Iridessa.

Silvermist's eyes darted over the water

as she tried to judge the distance to shore. It was too far for the girls to swim, and who knew what dangers lurked in the depths. But maybe there was another way. . . .

"Fawn," she said, "what do tortoises eat?"

"Plants, mostly," said Fawn.

"Like that seaweed?" Silvermist pointed to a large tangle of kelp floating on the surface of the water.

"That would be a tasty tortoise snack," Fawn agreed.

Silvermist nodded. "Okay. I have a plan."

Seconds later, the fairies flew to their tasks. Rosetta touched the seaweed with her garden magic so each leaf grew plumper and juicier. Iridessa made the seaweed glisten with sunlight to catch the tortoise's attention.

Meanwhile, Fawn buzzed around, trying to coax him forward.

The tortoise swiveled his head in the direction of the seaweed. He stretched his neck toward it.

Now came Silvermist's turn. With her water magic, she summoned a wave to 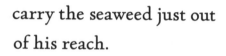 carry the seaweed just out of his reach.

Slowly, like an iceberg shifting, the tortoise moved toward the seaweed.

Each time he got close, Silvermist used another wave to pull the tempting snack away.

Wave by wave, the tortoise carried the girls closer to shore. "It's working!" Fawn cried. The other fairies cheered.

With a final surge, Silvermist sent the seaweed onto shore. The tortoise followed, pulling his heavy body half out of the water.

"Girls! Now!" Silvermist cried.

The girls leaped from his shell, dropping onto the wet sand below. The tortoise didn't seem to notice. He chomped the last bit of seaweed, hiccupped one more time, and then pushed himself backward into the water, sliding below the waves.

"We made it!" Lainey cheered. Mia and Gabby hugged each other, while the fairies fluttered happily around them.

Kate was the only one not celebrating. She bent over to pick something up from the sand.

It was a lunch box. The same one they'd found the day before.

"We didn't make it anywhere," Kate said, shaking her head. "We're right back where we started."

chapter 10

"Gah!" In a fit of frustration, Kate hurled the lunch box into the sea as far as she could throw it.

But it didn't sink. A wave carried it back to shore, depositing the box at her feet. *See?* it seemed to say. *It's useless to try to leave.*

"There has to be a way out of here," Lainey said. "We can find a way around the cliffs. Or . . . or the fairies can do some magic. Right?" She looked at them hopefully.

Fawn shook her head. "We need fairy dust to do magic. We just used ours up."

"You mean we're stuck here?" Gabby asked.

Mia turned to Kate. "This is *your* fault."

"Me?" Kate exclaimed. "What did I do?"

"*You* led us here," Mia snapped. "*You* said we should go to the castle. *You* wasted the fairy dust. And now we're going to be stuck here eating gross lunch-box leftovers forever!"

Kate wanted to say *That's not true.* But she couldn't. She *had* led them to the Lost Coast. She *had* urged them to the castle.

I didn't tell them the truth, Kate realized, thinking of the two-headed coin. She hadn't considered what was best for her friends. She'd only been thinking of getting her own way.

Kate looked at Lainey and Gabby. She wished they would say something to show they were still on her side.

They looked back at her with big, scared eyes. But neither one said anything.

When a child stops believing in fairies, a fairy disappears. That moment on the beach made Kate understand why. Her friends had stopped believing in her, and now she wanted to disappear.

"There's still one thing we haven't thought of," Silvermist said. "The troll said things leave the Lost Coast when they're found. Maybe someone will find us."

"But who's even looking?" Mia said

miserably. "Our parents won't miss us. Time always stops when we go to Never Land. And we didn't tell anyone in Pixie Hollow where we were going. How will they know where to find us?"

"I don't know," Silvermist said. "But it's our only hope."

There was nothing to do but wait. They sat in the sand, searching the empty sky, as minutes and hours ticked by.

To comfort herself, Kate looked through the treasures in her backpack. But now these, too, seemed like sad reminders of her failures.

During her first softball match, she'd fumbled a catch and lost the game.

And the library book. Kate thumbed unhappily through the pages. *Who keeps a library book for six months and never even bothers to read it?* she scolded herself.

Even Ellie's shiny button eyes seemed full of reproach. *You didn't take care. You lost me,* they seemed to say. Dear Ellie, her first best friend.

Was there anything she hadn't messed up? Kate thought back to their very first visit to Pixie Hollow, the first time they'd met the Never fairies. Kate had "borrowed" fairy dust to learn how to fly. But the truth was, she'd stolen it. So what if she'd been tricked into taking it by the fast-flying fairy Vidia? Kate herself had scooped it up, in the dead of night, and never stopped to ask whether it was okay.

And the return home had been no better. Clarion, queen of the Never fairies, had given Kate and her friends more fairy dust so they might fly back to Never Land one day. But they'd never had a chance to use it because Kate had lost that, too.

Kate's eyes suddenly went wide. *She'd lost that, too!*

"I know where we can find more fairy dust!" she cried, jumping to her feet.

Kate looked around the long coastline, and her heart dropped. The lost mittens and hats and balls and dolls seemed to stretch on for miles. What chance did they have of finding one tiny thing in that endless wasteland?

It's hopeless, Kate thought.

She took a deep breath. "No, it's not," she said aloud. "Not totally." Hope was the one thing they could not lose. Kate knew once it was gone, they might never find it again.

"Believe," she whispered. She picked up a kite and looked underneath it.

"Believe," Kate murmured as she dug through a pile of lost socks. *"Believe,"* she said louder. She peered inside a boot.

Her friends watched in alarm. "Has

Kate lost her mind?" Rosetta whispered.

"No." Kate straightened and faced her. "I got us into this mess, but I'm going to fix it. I lost a bag of fairy dust a long time ago. Remember?"

Kate watched her friends' expressions change from disbelief to understanding to dismay.

"We'll never find it," Mia said, looking around.

"You can believe what you want," Kate said. "I believe we will." She turned back to her search.

Gabby suddenly spoke up. "I believe, Kate," she said. She turned over a sand bucket and peeked inside.

"I do, too," said Silvermist. "I believe!"

She began to sift through a pile of loose buttons.

The others took up the chant. They looked in purses and underneath hubcaps. They dug through water bottles, homework, and umbrellas. Every time Kate wanted to give up, she reminded herself that there was only one choice. They could sit around waiting for someone to save them. Or they could try to save themselves.

"Believe!" Kate shouted.

She was concentrating so hard that when she finally saw the tiny bag, she almost didn't recognize it. It was sitting atop a crest of sand, looking much smaller than Kate remembered.

She plucked it up. It was the size of a peach pit, made of honey-colored velvet so soft Kate knew only Never fairies could have made it.

"It's here!" Kate cried. "I found it!"

Everyone raced to her and gathered around. Kate loosened the drawstring on the bag, and they all peeked inside. Fairy dust glittered back at them.

"But is it enough?" Mia asked. The fairy dust had been meant for the four girls only. Now they would need to share it with the four fairies, too.

"It will have to be. But . . ." Kate hesitated. She knew what they had to do. "We can't take anything with us. We'll have to leave all the toys behind."

The girls looked at the things they'd

lovingly collected. "Not even BowBow?" Gabby asked, squeezing her stuffed dog.

Kate shook her head. "Not even him."

With heavy hearts, the girls said good-bye to their old belongings. Lainey gave each stuffed animal a kiss. Mia combed her fingers through her favorite doll's hair.

Gabby hugged BowBow tight. "I won't forget you," she told him before adding him to the pile.

Kate tapped her softball for good luck and set it on the pile. She emptied the coins from her pockets. Then she picked up Ellie. She held her close to her face.

"You understand, don't you, old friend?" she whispered.

The little elephant smiled back at her.

Kate could have sworn she was saying yes.

She placed Ellie next to the other toys, then opened the bag of fairy dust.

One by one, the fairies and girls took pinches of fairy dust. Kate could tell they were holding back, taking the smallest amount. Even so, by the time it was Kate's turn, there was only a smidgen of fairy dust left.

Would it be enough?

Kate sprinkled the fairy dust over her head and shoulders. Almost at once, she felt the tingle that told her its magic was working.

"Ready?" she asked.

"Ready," Mia said. The others nodded.

They flew up, up, up, following the cliffs. A wind blew hard against them, as if it didn't want them to leave. Kate glanced over her shoulder as the beach receded beneath them.

At last, they landed atop the cliffs. As she touched down, Kate felt a lightness she hadn't felt all day. She didn't think it had anything to do with fairy dust.

Mia landed next to her. "I'm sorry for getting mad at you," she said.

"It's okay," Kate told her. "You were right. I did get us lost. I'm just glad we were able to find our way out."

They looked down at the beach below. From that great height, the piles on the beach looked like nothing more than trash.

"I know there's something down there that I want," Mia said. "But it's funny—all

of a sudden I can hardly remember what it is."

"I know what you mean," Kate said. She took one last look at the coastline below, then she turned and faced ahead.

They were standing at the edge of a great meadow. A stream wound through it like a silver ribbon. In the near distance, they could see a tall mountain.

A boulder sat near the meadow's edge. The rock was perfectly white, except for a small black smudge on one side.

Something about the spot drew Kate's attention. She moved closer to examine it.

"Everyone! Come quick!"

They all gathered around to stare at the mark on the rock. It read:

Tink was Here.